Foam Beetle

Inchworm

Hairwing Western
Green Drake

astern
Green Drake

San Juan Worm

Micro Egg

Bead Body Scud

Purple Parachute Adams

Sparkle Dun
March Brown

Pale Morning Dun

Light Cahill

Royal Wulff

Midge

RS2

Ian's Crunchy Caddis

Adams Wulff

Rubber Leg Stonefly

Stonefly Bugger

Beadhead Stonefly

DOWN BY THE RIVER

WITHDRAWN

A Family Fly Fishing Story

By Andrew Weiner

Illustrated by April Chu

Abrams Books for Young Readers
New York

Art's grandpa finished loading the fishing rods into the car.
"Let's be sure we've got all our gear," he said. "Boots, waders, vests . . ."

"Check," said Art.

"Rods, reels, fly boxes . . ."

"Check," said Art's mom.

"Lemonade, PB&J, apples, chocolate chip cookies."

"Check, check, check, check, " Art and his mom said together.

Grandpa laughed. "All set then. Everybody in!"

They climbed into the car—Mom behind the wheel, Grandpa beside her, Art in the back.

"I started taking your mom fishing when she was just a young girl," Grandpa said to Art as Mom drove.

Mom smiled. They were heading to the river. It was Art's favorite kind of day—a fishing day.

And he liked Grandpa's stories, too.

"Your mom was eight. Same age you are now, Art. She was a firecracker, all right."

It wouldn't be a long ride to the river. Art looked out the window as they passed the golden-leaved trees. Autumn had come, but the fishing was still good. Art could already picture a big trout on the end of his line.

"We fished this same river," said Grandpa. "Your mom had been asking to fish with me, watching me gather my tackle, looking over my shoulder as I tied flies, always asking questions. 'Which fly will you use? Elk Hair Caddis? Hare's Ear? Can I come?' I finally agreed to take her along."

They arrived at their favorite spot. "Made sense to learn from the man who knew, Dad. Still does," Mom said. "Looks like we've got the river to ourselves."

Soon they were assembling their gear: waders and boots, rods and reels. Then the air hummed with the sound of fishing lines being pulled through guides.

"On your eighth birthday I surprised you with your own rod and reel. Remember?" Grandpa said to Mom as they worked. "And waders and boots, just your size."

"Like these you gave me?" Art asked, shuffling a bit in his big boots.

"Yes, sir. And we came to this river, sat and talked, watched the water." Grandpa closed his eyes for a moment as he remembered. "Your mom picked the spot. And on the first cast—her very first—she caught a fish. What a beauty. And so was the fish!"

"Oh, Dad." Mom laughed, putting her arm around his shoulders.

Art looked at his rod. He'd never caught a fish on his first cast.

"Let's get the lay of the land," Grandpa said.

A big white bird flew overhead, patiently searching the river. "An osprey," Mom said. "He's here to fish, too."

The only sounds were the rustle of the leaves in the breeze and the gentle rippling of the stream as it flowed beneath overhanging branches and around rocks, curving around bends above and below where they stood. It was nearly as clear as a glass of water, and they could see the stones that lay below its surface.

Just then, there was a splash. "Looks like they're feeding," Grandpa said. "Could be a mighty fine day of fishing."

"Do you think so?" Art asked eagerly. He was imagining his first perfect cast and Grandpa's smile when he caught a beautiful fish.

A small bug with delicate wings landed on Art's arm. "A caddis," said Mom. "Trout food!"

The air was full of caddis. When they dropped into the water, hungry trout gobbled them up with a splash and a slurp. "They're feeding on top," said Grandpa.

Mom took a fly from her box and tied it to the end of her line, and then did the same for Art. "One of Grandpa's special Elk Hair Caddis. Fools 'em every time." She handed another to Grandpa. He tied it on almost faster than Art could see.

Mom slowly stepped into the
water, took a good look around,
and cast her fly.
  "Oh boy! Got one!"

"Same as always," Grandpa said with a chuckle. "She's a natural."

Mom slipped her net under the fish. She held the trout gently in the water, then raised it to show Art. "It's a rainbow," she said. He could see a beautiful red stripe along its silver side. She eased the fly out of the corner of its mouth and dipped the net into the water. The trout darted back into the river. "There she goes."

"Let's give your mom some space, Art. Those deep pools upstream always hold some beautiful fish." Art and Grandpa walked up the bank and stepped into the water. They pulled line from their reels. "You first," Grandpa said.

Art took a deep breath. The first cast. He lifted the line from the water, let it extend behind him, and cast it forward. The fly flew straight and true—right into a tree branch above the stream. Art looked over at Grandpa and wondered if he'd ever call him a natural.

Grandpa just smiled. "No worries, Art." He waded across the stream and pulled the fly free. "Let's move up to the next pool. I scared off any fish that were here."

They waded upstream together.

"Did I ever tell you the story of my first fishing trip?" Grandpa asked. "My brother took me along with some of his friends, and the first thing I did was hook my brother. On my very first cast, in front of everyone. Biggest thing I ever caught." He chuckled.

Art *had* heard the story before—lots of times—and it always made him smile. He took another deep breath and looked up the river. He saw a perfect spot by the far bank, a big rock fifteen feet away. Behind it was a section of slow, calm water. He was sure a trout would be there.

Art lifted his line again and it uncoiled behind him. He remembered everything he'd been taught: wrist firm, line extended back in a loop behind him without hitting the water, cast forward like driving a nail. The line arced forward and the fly landed softly a few feet above the rock. It drifted with the current past the rock. There was a splash and the line went tight. "Fish on!" said Grandpa. "Chip off the old block."

The rod bent. Art started to reel in the fish and felt the strong tug on the end of the line, the fish darting from one side of the river to the other and back again. "Easy does it," Grandpa said. When the fish got close, he reached into the water and put his hand beneath it to gently hold it still while he removed the hook. It came out easily, and Grandpa held the fish in the water for a moment more.

"It's a brown trout. You can tell by those beautiful spots on its side. Fourteen inches long, I'd guess. Good size fish, Art. Beautifully done." He released the fish and then put his arm around Art's shoulders and gave him a squeeze.

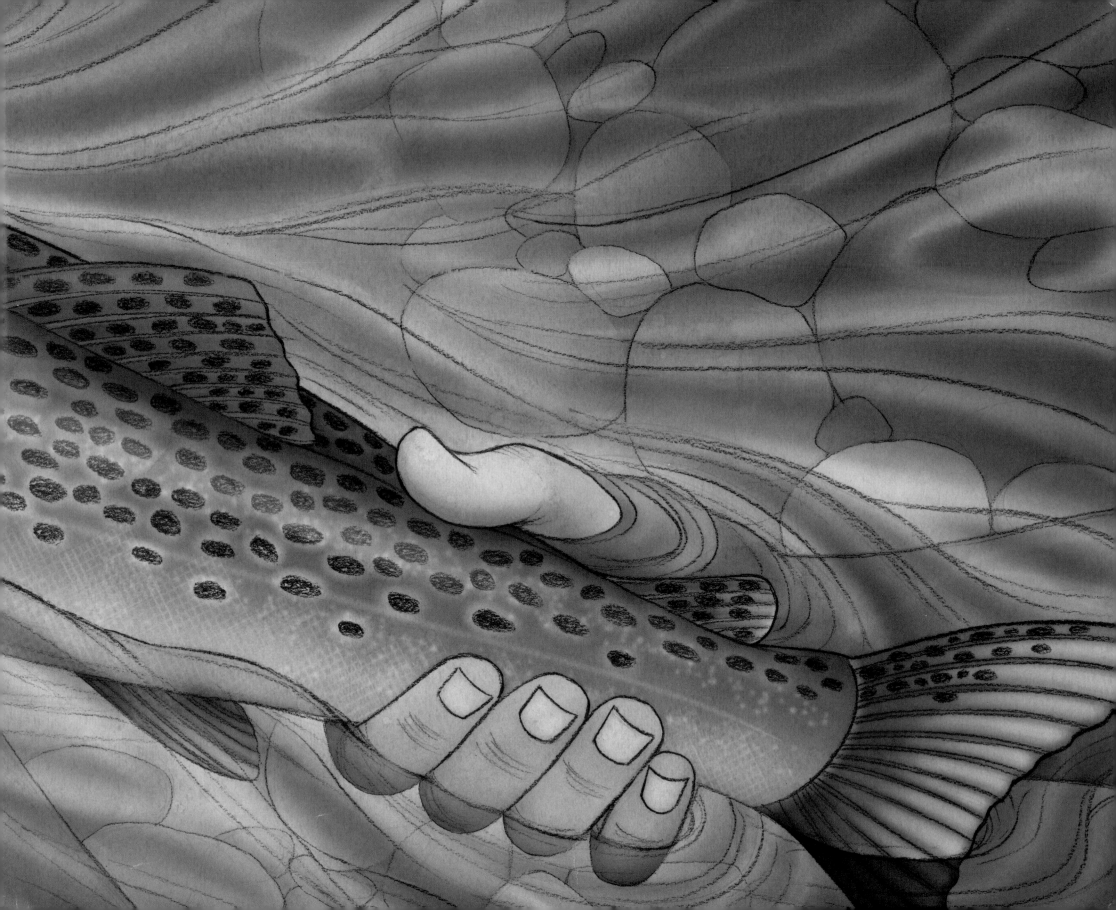

Overhead the osprey still circled, searching
for a trout of its own.

"You'll get one soon," Art called to the
bird. "Grandpa, one day I'm going to tell
my grandkids about fishing with you. I bet
we'll be fishing right here, and it will be as
nice as it is now."

"Just be sure to tell the good stories, Art.
Like this one." He smiled at Art, pulled him
close, and said, "Come on. Let's do it again.
Maybe it's my turn."

Art made a promise to himself.
I'll never forget this.

And he never did.

About Fly Fishing

Fly fishing is a way to catch almost any kind of fish, either in salt water, like oceans, or fresh water, like rivers and lakes. The flies are not the same flies that get into houses. They are artificial and created to imitate bugs, minnows, and other things on which fish feed. Sometimes these imitations look exactly like the real animal. Sometimes they don't. But when they float on top of the water or move beneath the water, fish *see* them as the real animal.

Fly fishing is different than other types of fishing, with lures or bait, because the fly isn't heavy enough to be cast on its own—it is the weight of the *fly line* that carries the fly forward. This sometimes requires the fly fisher, or angler, to apply a more precise motion to the fishing rod. Many anglers prefer the concentration and precision required by fly fishing, as well as the process of making many casts, and carefully observing the water for signs of fish.

How long has fly fishing been practiced?

Some believe that a type of fly fishing was practiced as early as the second century.

What is catch and release?

Releasing fish is a conservation method embraced by anglers that allows most fish to survive after being caught, so they can breed and produce more fish and be caught again. It helps to preserve a resource that is threatened and that is far smaller than it was in the past. In some areas it is prohibited to keep the fish you catch, while in others you can keep a maximum number of fish of a particular size. Be sure to find out what the rules and regulations are where you fish.

What is conservation?

Conservation is the preservation, protection, and restoration of the environment. Fish are a focus of conservation, as they live in rivers, streams, lakes, seas, and oceans—all of which can be damaged by pollution, improper use, and carelessness. Fish are often called bellwether species. This means that they can indicate the overall health of a watershed—the area around a river or a stream, a pond, or a lake. If fish are healthy, it is likely the watershed is healthy. If they are struggling to survive, chances are there are problems with the water, such as pollution. There are many individual anglers and angling groups that work to protect the environment. Some conservation groups are Trout Unlimited, Federation of Fly Fishers, American Rivers, The Nature Conservancy, The Wilderness Society, the Sierra Club, and California Trout.

What equipment is used to fly fish?

Flies

There are two basic types of flies. Dry flies float on top of the water. They can imitate grasshoppers, mice (yes, mice!), and different flying insects that either land on the water or rise to the surface as they go through their life stages. Sub-surface flies are called nymphs or streamers, and they imitate animals below the surface. These can be minnows, leeches, eggs (fish eggs or other animal's eggs), or nymphs (the early developmental stage of insects that hatch below the surface).

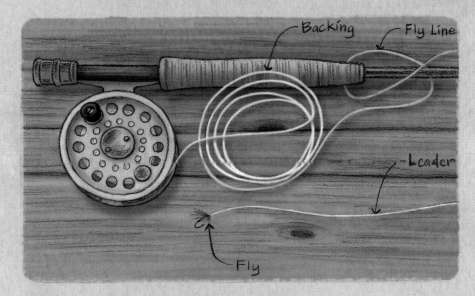

Fishing rod

Usually comes in several pieces that quickly fit together.

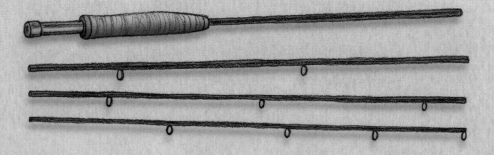

Reel

Holds three types of line:

Leader—the light and thin line to which the fly is tied

Fly line—a plastic-coated line that provides the weight necessary to cast a small and lightweight fly

Backing—the line that makes up the bulk of line on a reel. Its two purposes are to take up space on the reel and to provide additional line if a big fish begins to "run" (swim very strongly) and the leader and fly line are not long enough. (When a fish runs it is called "taking line" and is very exciting.)

Rods and reels come in various sizes and weights. The type of fish and the place one fishes determine how light or heavy the rod and reel should be.

What Do Anglers Wear?

Wading boots, which are made to be worn under water

Waders, which are worn over clothes to keep them dry and can go as high as the knee, waist, or chest

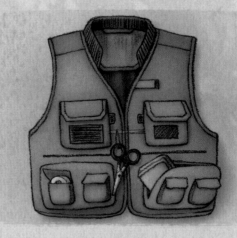

Vest, which has pockets to hold flies and other tools needed to fish

Net, to safely land a fish and protect it so it can survive being caught

Hat, sunglasses, and sunscreen, to protect from sunburn and heatstroke

A flotation device, to be worn while in a boat or wading

Are you interested in learning more about fly fishing and maybe trying it yourself?
Trout Unlimited and Federation of Fly Fishers both have clubs all around the country.

tu.org/connect/chapter-search

fedflyfishers.org/Councils/tabid/85/Default.aspx

To my father, Jack, for taking me fishing when I was a
boy and sharing trips as I got older. And to my mother,
Gloria, whose love of books gave me my passion and
my career.

—A.W.

For my mom

—A.C.

Acknowledgments

Thanks to my friend John Dally, who once said to me,
"That's not fly fishing. Get yourself a real fly rod and reel
and I'll meet you in Montana and we'll really fly fish."
Thank you for that trip, John.

And to the incredible book-selling community
that has been my home for forty years. And to Susan
Van Metre, in gratitude for taking on this project, and
working so tirelessly and kindly to make it a real book.

The illustrations in this book were created with charcoal pencil on paper, then
scanned and colored digitally.

Cataloging-in-Publication Data has been applied for and
may be obtained from the Library of Congress.
ISBN 978-1-4197-2293-6

Text copyright © 2018 Andrew Weiner
Illustrations copyright © 2018 April Chu
Book design by Julia Marvel

Printed and bound in China
10 9 8 7 6 5 4 3 2

Abrams Books for Young Readers are available at special discounts when
purchased in quantity for premiums and promotions as well as fundraising or
educational use. Special editions can also be created to specification. For details,
contact specialsales@abramsbooks.com or the address below.

ABRAMS The Art of Books
195 Broadway, New York, NY 10007
abramsbooks.com

Rattlin' Baitfish

TeQueely Streamer

Conehead Rubber Bugger

Orange Blossom Special Fly

Dave's Hopper

Foam Ant

Grannom Emerger

Letort Hopper

Stimulator

Renegade

Little Yellow Stonefly

March Brown Spider

Sedgehammer

Yellow Humpy

Goddard Sedge

Fluttering Blue Damsel

Royal Trude

PMX

Angel Wing Spinner

Slow Water Caddis